Little Douglas Fir

Story by Laurie Johnson

Illustrated by D.L. Sherwood

Early one wintry morning, a little Christmas tree

named Douglas Fir, stood on the top of a mountain.

The snow began to fall, and Douglas tried to catch the cold wet

snowflakes on the tips of his branches.

He was having a grand time. The air was cold and crisp and Douglas

could hear the wind whistling through the valley.

Suddenly, his fun was interrupted when
he heard a loud roar and felt the ground begin
to rumble beneath him.
Douglas looked down in horror as he saw
a huge truck filled with tied up Christmas trees.

"Oh no!," Douglas cried to himself,
"Why are they taking my friends away?"

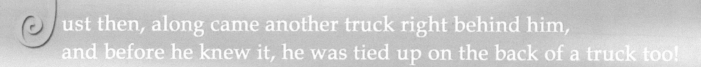

Just then, along came another truck right behind him,
and before he knew it, he was tied up on the back of a truck too!

Douglas shivered with fear as the
truck traveled down the long, winding road.
He felt scared and wondered what would become of him
as he watched his beautiful mountaintop home
disappear in the distance.

F inally, the truck stopped. A man got out and stood Douglas up and gave him some water. "There you go little tree," said the man as he began standing up all the other trees too.

"This water sure is good," Douglas said to himself, "Thank you, I was thirsty……but, where am I?"

s the sun continued to rise, people came to look at the trees…
lots and lots of people. Douglas was worried.
He missed his home on the top of the mountain.

"I wonder why they brought me here," Douglas thought to himself.

Just then, a young boy appeared in front of Douglas.

"Here it is, mom! Here's the one I want!" He yelled.

The boy's mother walked up. "Are you sure?" She said.

"It's not very big."

"Hey! Don't pick on my size, I could have grown plenty big
if those men would have left me on the mountain top!"

Douglas thought to himself.

All at once, Douglas was grabbed and tied up again, only this time, to the top of a car. "What's going on?" He wondered. "I want to go home I'm scared!"

Little Douglas Fir lay on top of the car and cried as the wind rushed through his branches.

After what seemed like forever,
the car finally stopped in front of a beautiful house
on the top of a mountain.

Douglas brushed away his tears as the boy and his father untied him from the car. He began to feel a little better as they carried him inside the beautiful house.

Inside it felt warm and cozy and smelled like pinecones.

Douglas could hear crackling and popping sounds coming

from the fireplace.

Suddenly a horrible thought crossed his mind,

"Firewood! They want me for firewood!

They're going to chop me up into little pieces and

throw me into the fireplace!" He cried.

He was terrified and began to shake.

Douglas closed his eyes tightly, "This is it, I'm going to be...."

T hen the boy and his father carefully set him down in front

of a big, lovely window that overlooked the city below.

Douglas smiled, "What a beautiful view!"

It reminded him of when he looked down from his mountaintop

home where he once stood.

"Maybe they like me! Maybe I can stay here for a while!"

As Douglas enjoyed the beautiful scenery from the mountain top window, his new family gave him some water and decorated him with the most beautiful lights and ornaments. There were strings of pearls, lace bows, lovely crystal icicles, sparkling white lights and garland.

Douglas' favorite decoration was a bright, shining star that was placed
at the very top of him. Douglas felt proud. He was beginning to
like this place and thought this family must like him too.
They all gathered around him and sang Christmas
carols as they placed beautifully wrapped
gifts under his branches.

L̲ittle Douglas Fir began thinking about his old home on the mountaintop. He thought about how frightened he was when the trucks came to take him away, and how scared he was when he was tied to the car. He thought about how terrifying this whole adventure had been and how he thought he'd been bought for firewood.

But Douglas knew one thing for sure; it was all worth it because it had led him to this lovely house on a beautiful mountaintop, to live with a wonderful family. He was so happy to share Christmas with them and he knew he made them happy too. Why, if he were still on the mountaintop, he would never have known about Christmas at all.

Christmas morning finally came, and the young boy rushed down the stairs

to find a stocking full of toys, games, books and treats,

all left by a jolly old man whom Douglas had never met before.

The boy's mother had been up all morning preparing for the exciting day.

There was eggnog, apple cider, muffins and cinnamon rolls, and a

whole table filled with other delicious looking treats.

Douglas was so happy to be a part of this day.
He loved watching the young boy light up as his family began to arrive.

There were grandparents, aunts, uncles and cousins.
They were all so happy to be together. There was so much love in the house.
Douglas felt warm as everyone gathered around him and
admired how beautiful he was.
They all opened their gifts and enjoyed one another's company.

Later that night, after much celebration, the young boy turned off Douglas' lights. It had been a long day and everyone was tired. Douglas was tired too. He closed his eyes and went to sleep.

Douglas enjoyed his new home and family for the next few days,
until early one morning when he was awakened by a loud noise.
He looked out the window and saw something that made his branches tremble!
A big garbage truck was picking up Christmas trees from some of
the nearby houses. "Oh no! Is this what's to become of me?
After all the happiness and joy I've felt here, now I'm to be tossed away?"
Douglas began to cry.

J ust then, the young boy came over and started removing all
of Douglas' beautiful lights and ornaments. Douglas was so sad.
He knew that tomorrow morning would be the end of him.
He worried and cried all night until morning came.

The sun came up and Douglas waited for the loud roar of the

garbage truck. He waited and waited, but it never came.

He began to wonder if the family would take him away themselves.

As he stood there not knowing what would happen,

the young boy and his father picked him up and took him outside.

Douglas waited to be tied to the top of the car once again.

But instead, the boy and his father began digging a hole.

"Oh, could it be?" Douglas wondered in excitement.

"Will they keep me here forever?"

They planted him right in the front yard of that grand house

on that beautiful mountaintop.

Now he would grow to be the biggest tree on the whole street.

Little Douglas Fir discovered that day just how much this family loved him.

Late that night, Douglas stood in the yard gazing up

at the billions of stars. He was happy, and had never felt more at home.

As the years passed, Douglas grew and grew

until he was the tallest tree in town.

Every year he was decorated at Christmas time, and people

would drive by just to see how beautifully lit up he was.

Douglas stood proudly in front of the grand house,

in the yard,

on that beautiful mountaintop,

which was now his home forever.

CPSIA information can be obtained
at www.ICGtesting.com
Printed in the USA
LVHW070258131220
674056LV00036B/244

9781505407839